PERSEUS & THE GORGON

Retold by Lesley Sims

Illustrated by Simona Bursi

Reading consultant: Alison Kelly
Roehampton University

Contents

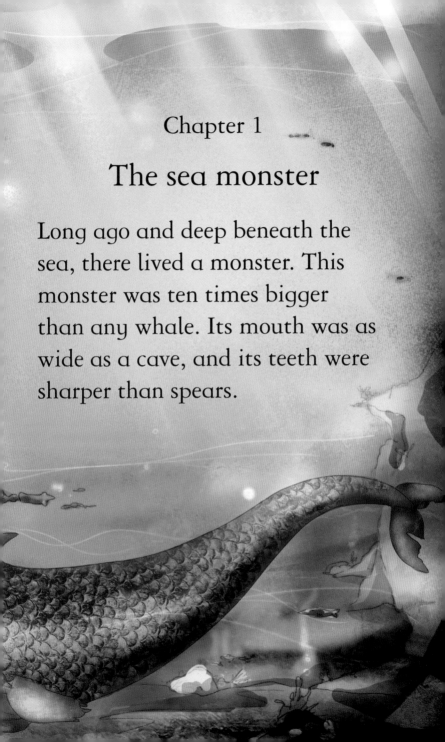

Chapter 1

The sea monster

Long ago and deep beneath the sea, there lived a monster. This monster was ten times bigger than any whale. Its mouth was as wide as a cave, and its teeth were sharper than spears.

For years, the monster prowled the deep sea near Ancient Greece. Feeding on sharks and giant squid, it was kept firmly under control by Poseidon, God of the Seas. But lately...

...the monster had been eating men.
Bursting from the depths, it
smashed through ships, scattering
fishermen into the water. Then it
gobbled them up with one snap
of its mighty mouth.

Villagers living near the sea were terrified of the monster, which they had named Cetus. They marched to the royal palace, calling to the king, "Cetus is killing our fishermen! Send your guards.

6

You must fight the monster!"

King Cepheus gazed down from his balcony with a worried frown. He had no idea how to save his people and his kingdom.

He went back to his throne, deep in thought. The monster was a menace, and it was all his wife's fault. She had boasted that their daughter, Andromeda, was more beautiful than the mermaids who served Poseidon – so Poseidon had let the monster go wild.

8

In desperation, King Cepheus consulted a priest. The priest's advice appalled him.

"There is only one way to pacify Poseidon. You must offer your daughter to the monster as a sacrifice."

The king and queen were grief-stricken. Andromeda, their young daughter, was horrified.

None of them knew that help was on the way – from a surprising young man.

Chapter 2

Perseus

The young man in question was currently in trouble and hiding from royal guards. His name was Perseus and the local king, Polydectes, wanted to marry his mother.

Unfortunately, his mother didn't want to marry the king. As they cowered behind their house, they heard the tramp of the king's guards approaching.

Are you in there? Come out NOW!

Perseus gave his mother a tight hug. "If we're quick," he said, "we can make it to the forest, where we can hide."

Tugging her hand, he raced down the street. But there were guards everywhere.

"Over there!" one of them yelled. "After them!"

Across the street, the village priest called to Perseus. "This way! I'll hide you!"

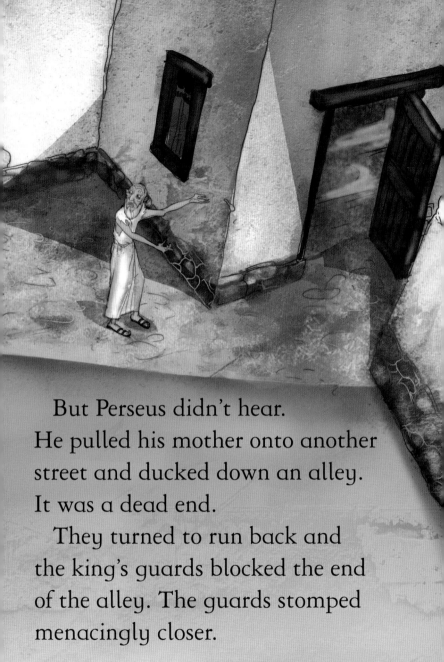

But Perseus didn't hear.
He pulled his mother onto another
street and ducked down an alley.
It was a dead end.

They turned to run back and
the king's guards blocked the end
of the alley. The guards stomped
menacingly closer.

Perseus stepped in front of
his mother. "Don't come any
closer," he warned the guards.

But they kept coming. "It's just
your mother we want," growled one.

14

Perseus hurled himself at the guards. He hoped to barge them over, so his mother could escape. The guards were too strong.

A fist crashed against his head, and he fell to the ground.

"Tell the king I'll do anything he wants if he leaves my mother alone," Perseus cried. "I'll even bring him the head of Medusa herself."

The guards laughed in disbelief.

Medusa was a Gorgon, a monster so ugly that just one glance at her face turned men to stone.

"We'll tell him," said the guards, as they dragged his mother away.

Perseus tried to lift himself up. "I'll fetch Medusa's head," he promised his mother, "and I'll use it to turn King Polydectes to stone."

Then pain overwhelmed him and his eyes fluttered shut.

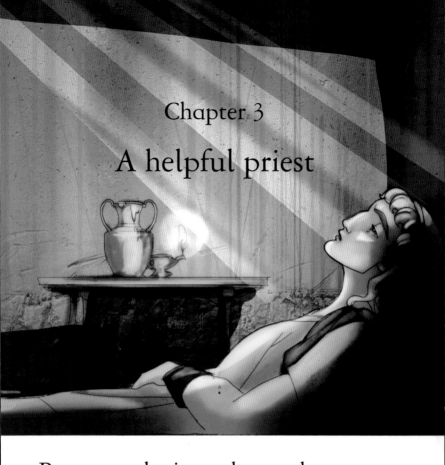

Chapter 3

A helpful priest

Perseus woke in a gloomy house. Daylight shone through cracks in the walls, dazzling his bleary eyes.

"Ah, you're awake," said a voice.

"Huh?" said Perseus, struggling to sit up.

The village priest was watching him. "Aagh..." Perseus moaned, as pain shot through his head. "What happened?"

"I heard what you said about Medusa," said the priest. "But you were in no state to fight anything, so I brought you here."

"Now," he went on, "there are some things you need to know. First, your real father..."

"I don't know who he is," Perseus interrupted, "I've never met him."

"I'm not surprised," the priest replied. "It's Zeus, the King of the Gods."

Perseus was astounded. "Zeus? Then I'm half a god! King Polydectes won't be able to stop me. I must go to the palace and rescue my mother at once."

But the priest sprang in front of him, blocking the door.

"Fool!" he said. "The palace has a hundred guards. There's no way you can defeat them on your own, whoever your father was."

"No," he added, "you must do as you promised your mother. Find Medusa, then come back and turn her head on the king."

Perseus looked doubtful. "Even if I am Zeus's son," he said, "how can I defeat Medusa? Some of the country's bravest warriors have tried and failed."

"The gods will send gifts to help," said the priest.

As he spoke, a razor-sharp sword and shimmering shield appeared.

"The sword will cut anything," he explained. "And if you only look at Medusa's reflection in the shield you will be safe." He handed Perseus a leather bag. "For her head," he added, grimly. "Now, go to the forest and seek the three witches. Only they know where Medusa lives."

Chapter 4

Witches of the forest

Perseus made for the forest as fast as he could. His shield was heavy, and the sword swung awkwardly from his belt. But he needed both to stand any chance of catching the wicked Medusa.

First, though, he had to find the witches.

Reaching the forest, Perseus crept inside. The wind whispered in the trees, and only a few lonely shafts of sunlight pierced their tangled branches. But there was another light up ahead – firelight.

Three wrinkly old witches sat
around a bubbling cauldron.
Perseus shuddered when he saw
that they had no eyes, only empty
sockets, dark and dead inside.

One of the witches sprang up. "Who's there?" she shrieked.

Rummaging in her pocket, she pulled out a slippery eyeball. She slotted it into her eye socket and glared at Perseus across the fire.

"Oooh," she said. "A warrior."

"Let me see!" snapped another of the witches. She plucked the eyeball from her companion's face and shoved it into her own.

"Oooh," she cooed. "He's got lovely eyes."

"Give me that!" demanded the third witch, snatching the eyeball.

As she peered at Perseus, her shrivelled mouth spread into a nasty grin.

"Oooh," she gurgled. "He has lovely *shiny* eyes."

"Enough!" Perseus said. "I seek the Gorgon Medusa."

The witches began to cackle. "Medusa!" they shrieked. "He seeks Medusa! No one ever makes it out of Medusa's cave alive."

"Cave?" Perseus said. "Which cave? Tell me!"

"Ah," said the third witch, "but there is a price for that information."

"What price?"

The witch stepped closer, grinning hideously. "Your lovely eyes," she said.

These old hags were crazy, Perseus thought, but he needed their help. "Very well," he said, sliding out his sword. "I will give you my eyes."

The witches scuttled closer, drooling with excitement. "Let *me* see. Give *me* the eye!"

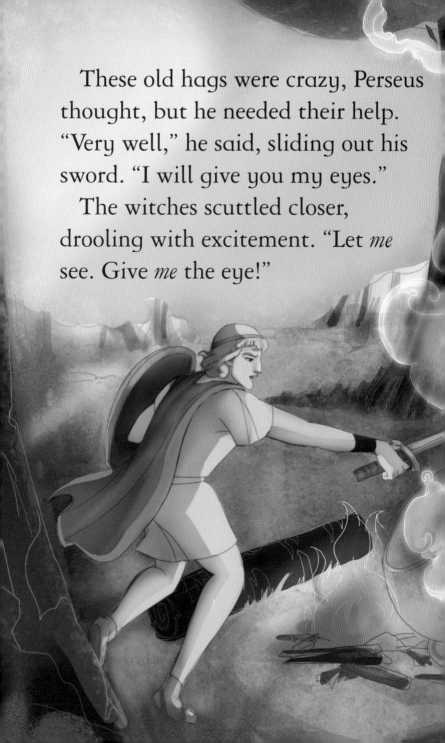

Fast as a flash, Perseus lashed
out his sword and knocked the
cauldron onto the fire. A cloud of
steam hissed at the witches' faces.

The witches staggered back, dropping the eyeball to the ground. Perseus snatched it up and held it in his palm.

"I have your eye," he said. "Now, tell me where Medusa lives or I'll squash it like a bug."

"Tell him!" the witches shrieked. "Tell him! Tell him!"

"She lives in a cave."

"Which cave?" Perseus demanded.

"Beneath the Black Mountain.
The Cave of the Dragon's Mouth."

Satisfied, Perseus tossed them the
eyeball. Then he turned and raced
from the forest.

"You'll die warrior!" the witches
shrieked. "Everyone dies in
Medusa's cave!"

Chapter 5

The Dragon's Mouth

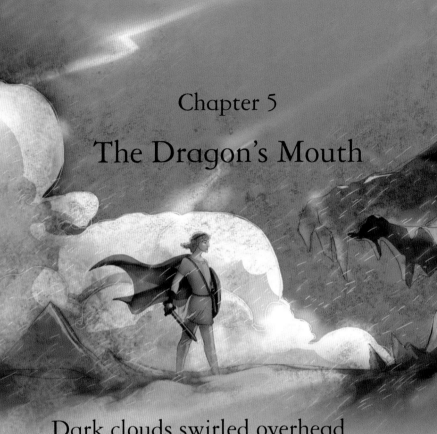

Dark clouds swirled overhead
as Perseus emerged from the forest.
A flash of lightning streaked across
the sky. Perseus was tired and cold,
but he kept going until he reached
a slope of dark rocks – the
Black Mountain.

Jagged stalactites hung from the
entrance to a cave, like the fangs
of some terrible beast. This was the
Cave of the Dragon's Mouth. This
was where Medusa lived.

Perseus's grip tightened around
his sword. He tried to stop himself
from trembling.

The cave grew colder as he crept inside. In the dim light he saw strange rock shapes, like statues of men. No, he realized with a shudder... They *were* men.

These were the warriors who had
tried to kill Medusa. They had all
been turned to stone by her snakes.
Frozen faces leered from the dark,
mouths open in silent screams, and
eyes wide with terror.

Deeper in the cave, something moved. Quickly, Perseus hid behind one of the stone warriors. A loud hiss echoed around the cave.

Don't look, Perseus told himself. If he looked at Medusa, he would be turned to stone too.

But just because he couldn't look at Medusa, didn't mean he couldn't *see* her. He raised his shield, and there she was in the reflection.

The Gorgon had a long, wormy body and lethal-looking claws.

Dozens of snakes writhed on her head, snapping and hissing and baring their vicious fangs.

Suddenly, the snakes turned and glared at where Perseus was hiding. They had seen him!

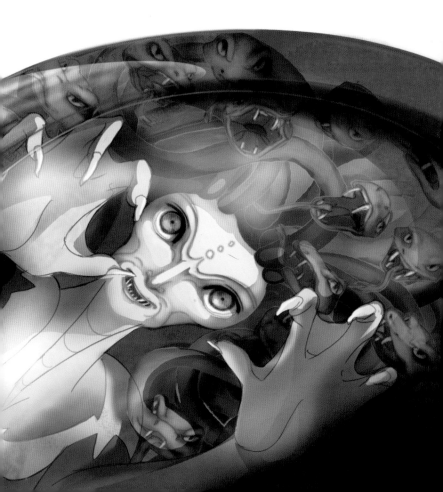

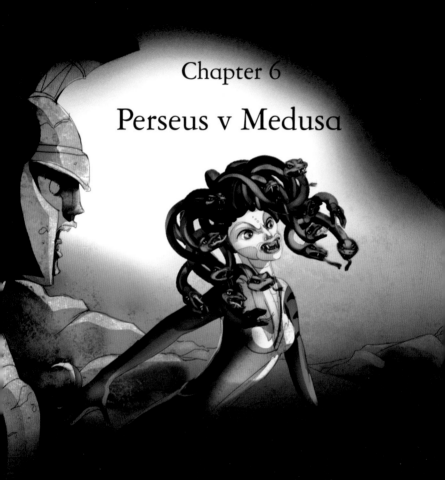

Chapter 6

Perseus v Medusa

Perseus's heart raced as Medusa slithered closer. In his shield, he saw the snakes on her head wriggle and writhe.

"Warrior," they hissed. "Look at us, warrior. Look at us and it will all be over."

No, Perseus thought. If he looked at them, he'd be turned to stone. He had to strike fast and catch Medusa by surprise.

Gathering his courage, he burst from his hiding place. He held his shield up high and whirled his sword at the Gorgon.

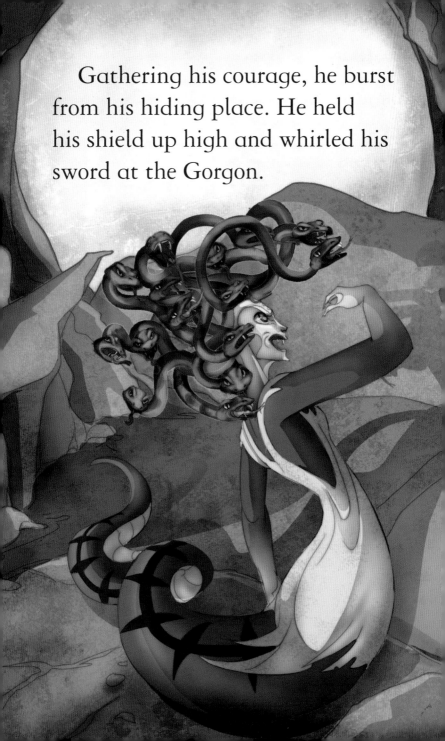

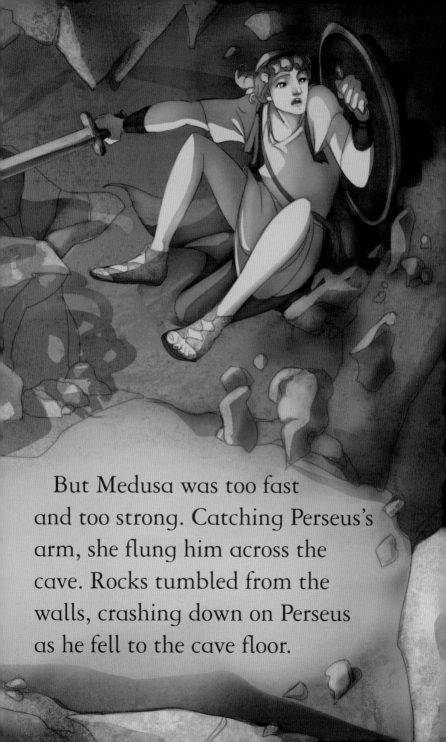

But Medusa was too fast
and too strong. Catching Perseus's
arm, she flung him across the
cave. Rocks tumbled from the
walls, crashing down on Perseus
as he fell to the cave floor.

Perseus tried to scramble up, but his legs were trapped. He couldn't reach his sword. In his shield, he saw Medusa approach.

"Look at us warrior..." the snakes hissed. "Look..."

Perseus stared at the hideous face in horror as it came ever closer and closer.

The monster grasped Perseus's back, roughly turning him over. Perseus tried to fight her, but she had the strength of one hundred warriors.

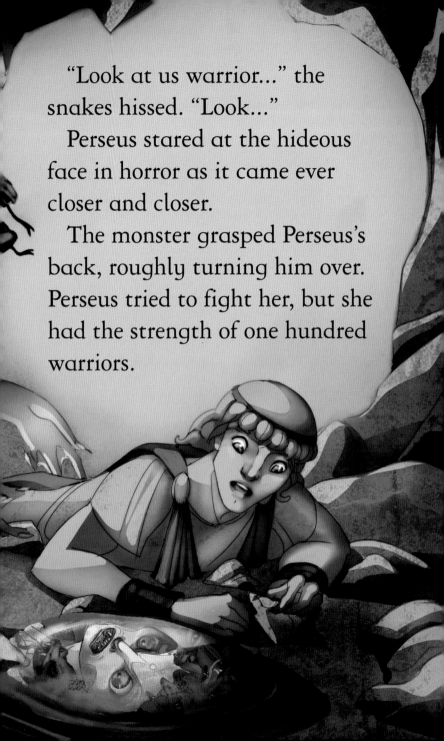

At once, he shut his eyes. Feeling around, he grabbed hold of a rock, swung it forward and rammed the jagged edge into Medusa's hand.

Medusa gave a piercing scream. Perseus twisted from her grasp. Then, looking only at the ceiling, he hurled the rock at a stalactite.

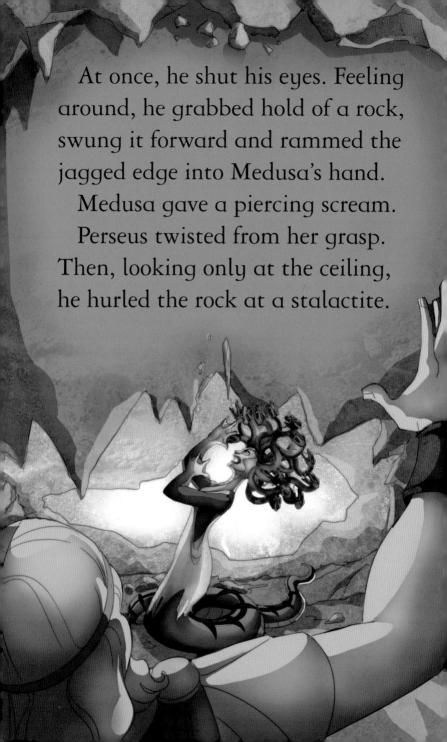

The stalactite cracked. It shot
down towards Medusa, slicing her
head straight off.

Perseus dragged himself to the
shield and saw the severed head's
reflection. She was dead. To his
relief, the snakes still hissed and
spat. He prayed they could still
turn King Polydectes to stone.

Making sure to keep his eyes
firmly shut, Perseus placed the
head in his leather bag. He ached
all over, but there was no time to
rest. Perseus turned and staggered
from the cave.

Chapter 7

Attack of
the sea monster

The storm grew stronger as Perseus
struggled back towards the coast.
Icy rain lashed against his face,
and fierce winds threatened to tear
the bag from his hands. But he
held on tight, feeling the snakes on
Medusa's head wriggle inside.

He was well on his way when he saw a crowd gathered at the top of a cliff in the distance, staring out to the stormy sea. Perseus was puzzled. What was going on?

Then he saw a beautiful woman at the bottom of the cliff, being chained to a rock. With one glance at her face, he fell in love.

High above her, a man stood watching the scene, looking heartbroken. It was the day of Andromeda's sacrifice.

Perseus watched. A dark shape
rose from the depths of the sea.
"Cetus!" screamed the crowd.

The monster's long fangs flashed in a streak of lightning as it swam forward. It had seen Andromeda, and it was hungry.

Perseus didn't know who they were but he knew he could rescue the girl. He reached for his bag, feeling Medusa's head inside. If he could just get this monstrous creature to look at the snakes...

Charging for the edge of the cliff,
he leaped from the end.
He fell...
   and fell...
      landing hard on
         the monster's back.

With a cry, he plunged his sword
into Cetus's shoulder. The monster's
roar was louder than thunder. It
thrashed and rolled, trying to
shake Perseus off. But Perseus
clung on tight to his sword. He was
waiting for the right moment...

"Now!" he thought.

Just as the sea creature lurched forward, Perseus let go of his sword, so he was flung high in the air and into the water.

Bursting to the surface, he swam frantically for the rocks. The monster came after him, its vast mouth wide open.

With the last of his strength, Perseus hauled himself onto the rocks. "Shut your eyes!" he yelled to the girl. "Don't look!"

He reached into his bag and pulled out Medusa's head. Closing his own eyes, he thrust the grisly trophy into the air.

The monster glared furiously at the hissing snakes. Its mouth opened to roar, but no sound came out. It looked down, horrified to see its body turning to stone. But still it came after Perseus. It was moving slower and slower, but it was getting closer and closer…

The girl cried out. Perseus dropped the head and put his arms around her. The monster's shadow fell over them. Its huge mouth opened… but it didn't shut. It stood as silent and still as the cliffs. It had turned entirely to stone.

With his eyes shut again, Perseus
felt for Medusa's head and put it in
his bag, before returning to the girl.

"You saved my life!" she said.
"And I don't even know your name."

"Perseus," gasped Perseus, still
getting his breath back.

"Thank you, Perseus. I'm Princess
Andromeda," she replied. "My
father is on top of the cliffs. I'm
sure he'll want to thank you too."

As Perseus helped Andromeda up the cliff, the villagers roared and cheered in delight.

King Cepheus beamed when he was introduced to Perseus. "You must celebrate with us," he said.

"I would love to," said Perseus, gazing at Andromeda, "but I have some unfinished business first."

"Come back when you can," said the king.

"I'll be waiting," Andromeda added, with a shy smile.

Perseus's mother gasped with relief when her son strode into the throne room up to King Polydectes.

The king was astounded to see Perseus actually return with Medusa's head. But he didn't say a word. He had leaped from his throne and now stood in silence, totally still – as still as a statue.

Usborne Quicklinks

For a pronunciation guide to the Greek names
in this book, and links to websites where you can
find out more about Greek myths and life in Ancient
Greece, go to **www.usborne-quicklinks.com**
and enter the keyword 'Perseus'.

When using the internet please follow the internet safety guidelines
displayed on the Usborne Quicklinks Website. The recommended
websites in Usborne Quicklinks are regularly reviewed and updated,
but Usborne Publishing Ltd is not responsible for the content or
availability of any website other than its own. We recommend
that children are supervised while using the internet.

History consultant: Dr. Anne Millard

Designed by Michelle Lawrence
Additional design: Emily Bornoff
Digital design: Nick Wakeford

First published in 2011 by Usborne Publishing Ltd.,
83-85 Saffron Hill, London EC1N 8RT, England.
www.usborne.com Copyright © 2011 Usborne Publishing Ltd.